For Ben c.h.

For Mum and Dad, with love c.w.

CIP Data is available.

First published in the United States 1994
by Dutton Children's Books,
a division of Penguin Books USA Inc.
375 Hudson Street, New York, New York 10014

Originally published in Great Britain 1994
by Magi Publications, Middlesex, England.
Typography by Amy Berniker

First American Edition
ISBN 0-525-45340-7
1 3 5 7 9 10 8 6 4 2
Reprinted by arrangement with Dutton Children's Books,
a division of Penguin Books USA Inc.
Printed in the U.S.A.

Oliver All Alone

Oliver All Alone

by **Christine Harris**

illustrated by **Catherine Walters**

DUTTON CHILDREN'S BOOKS

New York

Oliver stood in the hall with his leash in his mouth and watched as his family walked out the front door.

"Sorry, Oliver," said Mom. "We're going to visit Grandma for Christmas Eve, and they don't allow puppies in the hospital. We'll be back soon."

Oliver heard the *crunch crunch* of their footsteps on the snow and the slam of the car doors.

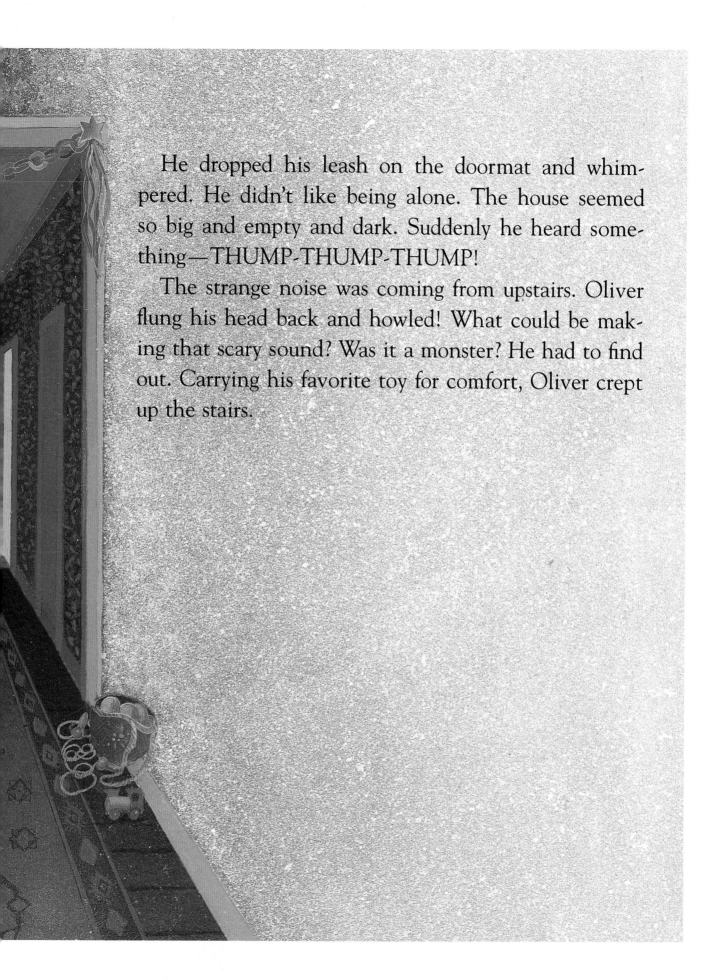

He dropped his leash on the doormat and whimpered. He didn't like being alone. The house seemed so big and empty and dark. Suddenly he heard something—THUMP-THUMP-THUMP!

The strange noise was coming from upstairs. Oliver flung his head back and howled! What could be making that scary sound? Was it a monster? He had to find out. Carrying his favorite toy for comfort, Oliver crept up the stairs.

He prowled along the landing with his tummy close to the carpet and peered into Mom and Dad's bedroom. There on the bed sat a bulging, stringy-tailed beast!

"*Grrh*," growled Oliver as fiercely as he could. He launched his small body at the stringy-tailed monster, snarling as he shook it to bits. Just when he was feeling very proud of himself, he heard another THUMP-THUMP-THUMP! But now the noise was coming from somewhere else.

Oliver raced to the window, stood on his hind legs, and looked out. A tall white stranger stared up at him.

Oliver barked and scratched at the window. If only he could get outside and chase the stranger away. He barked and barked, but the figure didn't budge.

The little dog was making so much noise that he almost didn't hear the THUMP-THUMP-THUMP! This time it was coming from behind him!

With a surprised yelp, Oliver skedaddled down the stairs, heading for the safety of his blanket in the kitchen. But between him and his bed, a huge lumpy shape crouched on the kitchen table.

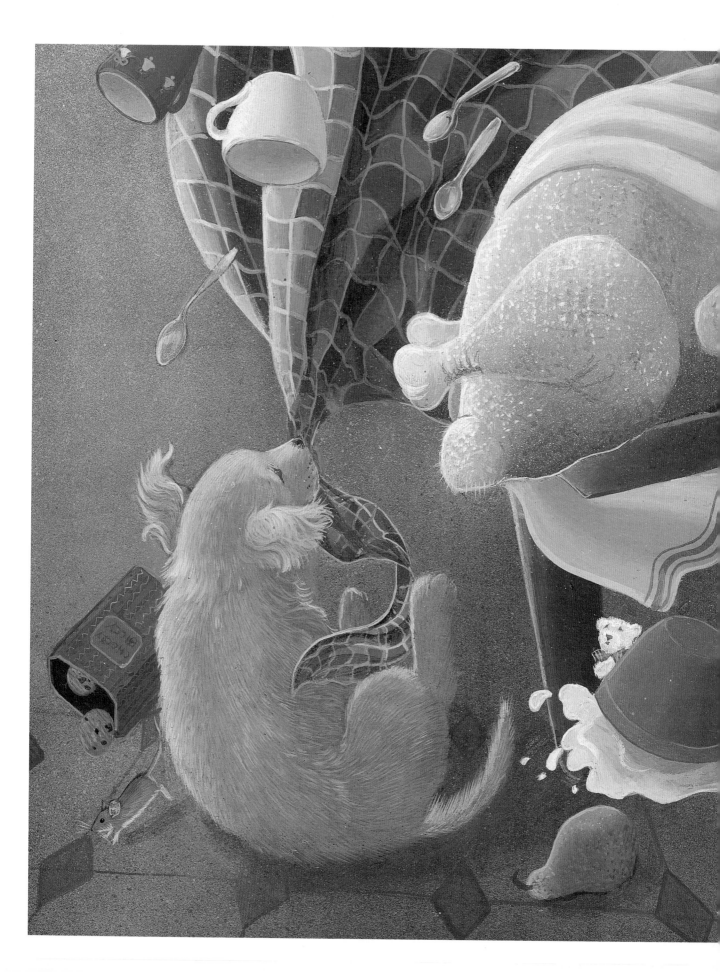

Before the creature could spring on top of him, Oliver decided to pull it down from its perch. He grabbed one end of the tablecloth and tugged with all his might. The lumpy thing tumbled to the floor.

Oliver butted it with his nose. It felt as cold as ice and as hard as stone, but it smelled good...THUMP-THUMP-THUMP! The noise interrupted Oliver's inspection.

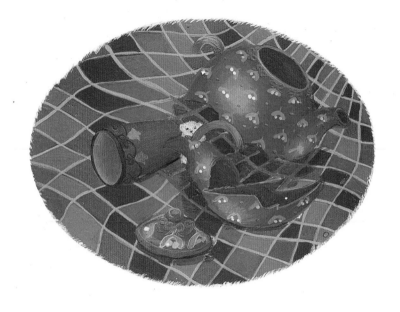

The puppy crept out of the kitchen and into the family room. There beside the funny tree with the blinking lights lurked a fat, wrinkled creature. It frowned at Oliver but didn't move.

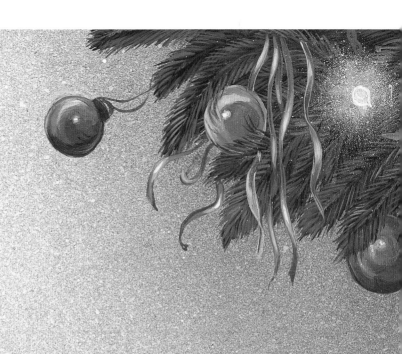

So Oliver pounced, and the creature fell sideways. Its mouth opened, and its long, slippery arms wrapped around him. Oliver bit and pulled at them until he managed to struggle free.

THUMP-THUMP-THUMP!

That noise again! Now it was coming from the living room.

This time Oliver was determined to find out what was making the thumping sound. Being careful not to alert the intruder, the puppy inched quietly toward the living room door. A strange shadow moved along the wall. Oliver had caught the thumping creature at last! Barking furiously, he raced into the room…

…and found a nice smiling man, not a monster at all.

"I'm early tonight," said the visitor. "It looks like everyone is out, except you. Did they leave you to guard the house? Well, you're very brave to come rushing in like this."

Oliver wagged his tail but felt a little sheepish.

The man chuckled and said, "I have a special reward for good dogs like you." He pulled a big bone from his sack and gave it to the excited puppy.

Just then, Oliver heard the front door open…

"Oliver, we're back!"

Oliver bounded into the hall, and there was his family, home at last!

"Why, Oliver," they cried, "who gave you that bone?"

But Oliver just thumped his tail on the floor—THUMP-THUMP-THUMP!